DATE DUE

AUG 2 7 2003		
NOV 3 0 2004		
JUL 2 4 2006		
AUG 0 9 2012		
AUG 2 9 2012		
APR 2 0 2013		
MAY 2 0 2013		
JAN 2 8 2015		
	DISCARDED	
GAYLORD		PRINTED IN U.S.A.

ERNEST
THE FIERCE MOUSE

Amy and Philip Rowe

Illustrated by Andrea Norton

FOREST HOUSE

REINFORCED LIBRARY BINDING

This is a story
about a mouse
named Ernest.

Ernest lived in a small hole
in the wall of a little red house
with a beautiful garden.

Ernest was a fierce mouse.
This is unusual because
most mice are very quiet and shy.

One sunny morning Ernest the
fierce mouse was walking among
the garden flowers. It was warm and
Ernest stopped to sniff the flowers.

He looked carefully around him.
He looked behind a red flower.
He looked behind a clump of
green grass. Nobody was there.
"Good," said Ernest.

He said "good" because on
sunny days Ernest liked to turn
cartwheels. He took a big breath
and threw himself into the air. He
landed with a bump and then dusted
himself off.

"Good," said Ernest and did another
cartwheel. But this time
he went too far and landed on
the long arm of a rose bush.
"Ouch!" said Ernest. "I don't like
thorny plants!"

"Next time keep your long arms
out of my way."
The rose bush moved its arms slightly.
"Good," said Ernest, angry because
the rose bush had seen him doing his
cartwheels. The morning was spoiled.

He set off for home, dragging his
tail behind him.
But suddenly he stopped.
On the path in front of him
was a footprint.
And it was *enormous*!

Next to it there was another…
and another…
Somebody, or something, was
walking in his garden. Ernest
the fierce mouse followed
the footprints.

Soon he met a spider.
"Have you been walking in my
garden?" said Ernest fiercely
to the spider.
"It wasn't I," said the spider in
a silky voice. "It was a monster."

"Monster!" said Ernest. "I'm not
afraid of monsters."
And he went on following
the footprints.

Before long he found a long,
orange tail sticking out from
under a bush.
It was the cat.

"Why are you hiding under that bush?" said Ernest fiercely.

"Who's that?" said the cat. "Is that
the monster?"
"No," said Ernest. "What monster?"
"There's a monster, a monster in
the garden," the cat whispered.

"Monster!" said Ernest. "I'm
not afraid of monsters!"
The cat hid under his bush
again, and Ernest followed the
footprints further.

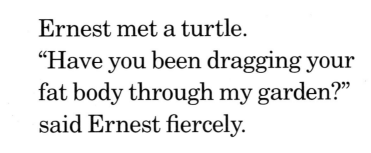

Ernest met a turtle.
"Have you been dragging your
fat body through my garden?"
said Ernest fiercely.

"Not I," said the turtle, yawning,
"I've been asleep all morning."
"I suppose it must have been the
monster," said Ernest. "Well, I'm
not afraid of monsters!"

The footprints came to an end…
and there…
under the bushes…was the monster.

"Well," said Ernest fiercely.
"Why have you been walking
through my garden?"

The monster was silent.
"What kind of monster are you if
you can't even talk?" cried Ernest.
The monster said nothing.

"Look," said Ernest, "this is my garden and I don't allow monsters in. You'll have to go." There was a cracking sound.

Ernest hid behind a flower…
to see better.
"Monster!" he shouted. "You don't
frighten me! I'm Ernest the fierce
mouse!"

The cracking sound grew louder,
until with one final crack, the
monster threw off its coat, and ran
squeaking through the garden.
The monster was gone.

Ernest went back along the path.
He met the turtle.
"I frightened the monster," said
Ernest. But the turtle didn't
hear because he was asleep.

Ernest found the cat, still hiding
under the bush. "Who's there?"
said the cat in a frightened voice.
"It's me, Ernest the fierce
mouse!" replied Ernest.
"Mouse?" asked the cat.
"And I frightened the monster!"
added Ernest.
"Oh," said the cat, nervously, and
disappeared under his bush.

Ernest met the spider.
"Did you find the monster?" asked
the spider.
"I did," replied Ernest. "And I
frightened it off."

"Oh, you are clever," said the
spider.
"Of course I am. I'm Ernest the
fierce mouse."
Ernest felt it was time for lunch.

He went back along the path.
He smiled to himself and said proudly,
"I am the fiercest animal in the garden,
even the monster ran away from me."

He was so happy he felt like doing a cartwheel.
He stopped and looked around. Then, well away
from the rose bush, he turned a gigantic cartwheel…

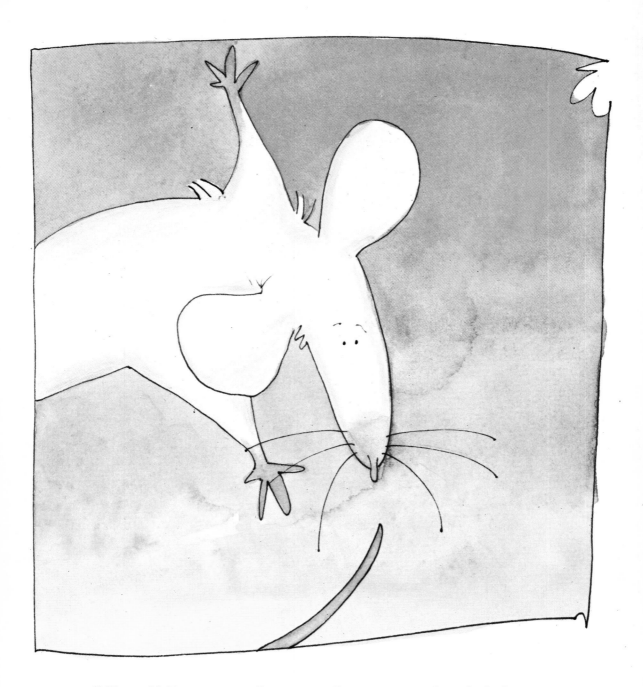

"Good! It turned out to be a wonderful day
after all," said Ernest,
and he turned another cartwheel.

This edition first published in the United States in 1990 by Gallery Books, an imprint of W.H. Smith Publishers, Inc. First published in the United Kingdom in 1985 by William Collins Sons and Co. Ltd. Produced for Gallery Books by Joshua Morris Publishing, Inc. in association with William Collins Sons and Co. Ltd. Text copyright © 1985 by Amy and Philip Rowe. Illustrations copyright © 1985 by Andrea Norton. All rights reserved. ISBN 0-8317-4455-3. Printed in Hong Kong.